For all my family and especially Lucas, Émanuel and Rébéca.
Thank you, Marty, for your support.
T. D.

Leon the Raccoon
Discovers the World

Text by Lucie Papineau
Illustrations by Tommy Doyle

AUZOU

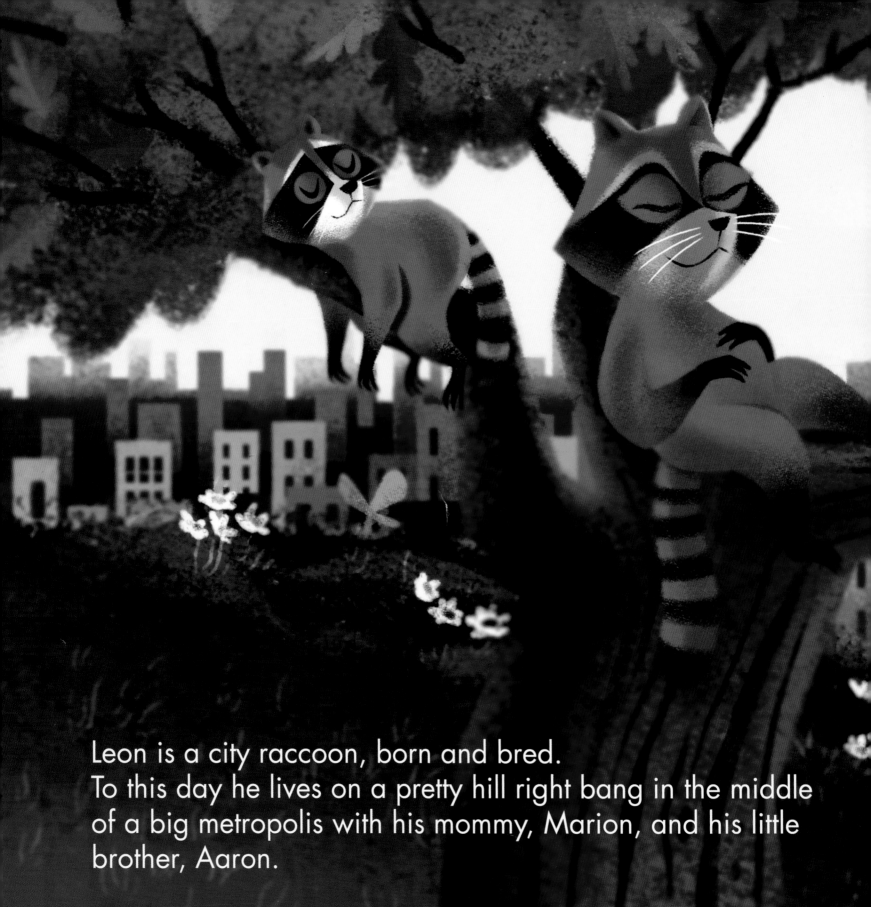

Leon is a city raccoon, born and bred.
To this day he lives on a pretty hill right bang in the middle
of a big metropolis with his mommy, Marion, and his little
brother, Aaron.

Like all raccoons, Leon sleeps during the day.
But, as soon as it's dark, he scoots off with
his friends for a night of fun and adventure
in the city!

Leon never gets bored. There's always something
to do in this huge playground… his city!

One fine evening, while his little family is watching
the city light up, Mommy Marion has an idea.
"Let's go visit our cousins… in the country!"

Leon is horrified. He's not interested in meeting his country cousins. After all, everyone knows that country raccoons are very different from city raccoons. They don't know anything about anything!

Yet here is our little friend, tucked inside a truck with his little brother and his mommy, headed to the great unknown.

The truck soon starts lurching and rolling...
it's going to be a bumpy ride!

The journey seems endless and Leon cannot get to sleep. He peeks out of the truck to discover they have turned off the highway onto a narrow road. Before long, they are driving along a dirt path...

The landscapes flicks by like the pages of a cartoon flipbook. Leon can see huge animals grazing in the field—swishing their tails to keep the flies away—and trees, a babbling brook, and butterflies, fluttering from flower to flower.

As soon as the truck stops and the driver walks away,
the little family climbs down and tiptoes away.

Soon, they meet their country cousins waiting for them on the bank of a brook. Leon's mother gives her sister, Sharon, a warm hug. As for Aaron, he seems delighted to meet his cousins, Jason and Alison.

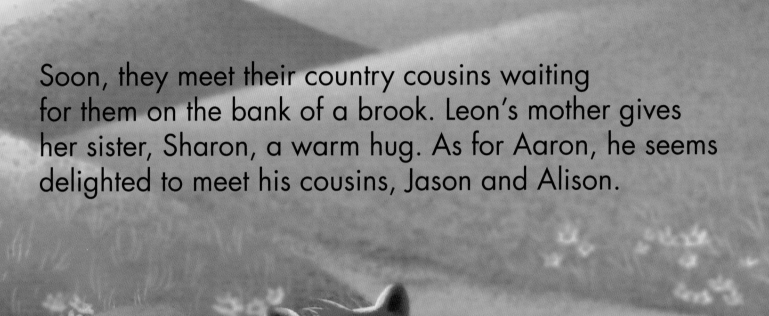

Leon, on the other hand, walks away without a word.

Even when he hears strange noises
Even when weird insects buzz around his ears.
Even when he is afraid of his own shadow...
Leon is determined to sulk.
All. Night. Long.

Soon, however, Leon starts feeling lonely.
From a distance, he can hear everyone else laughing
and singing. So, when cousin Alison comes to fetch him,
he immediately jumps to his feet.

All the raccoons have gathered together on the edge of a glade around a campfire. Wow! The flames seem to be dancing in the night... Leon has never seen anything like it!

The little raccoons admire the embers glowing in the dark. Jason is delighted. He has sniffed out a bag of marshmallows that someone left behind!

Leon's cousin threads a marshmallow onto a twig and grills it over the fire. The marshmallow slowly puffs up and turns a delicious golden brown. Yummy!

One by one the stars begin to twinkle in the night sky. Leon thinks of home and the city lights shining brightly in the night. The view may be quite different here but it is just as wonderful.

The little raccoon looks at his cousins, Jason and Alison. They may not be like his city friends but it is certainly not true that they don't know anything about anything.

Alison knows the names of almost all the stars in the sky...
and Jason builds the most awesome campfires!

about his many journeys and tells wonderful stories of what he has seen: the oceans, huge mountains, seemingly endless pine forests, wild bears...

Leon drinks up every word, wide-eyed.
He, for sure, has never seen anything like that!

His mind is made up!
When he grows up, he will be an explorer!
He will travel to places where no raccoon
has ever set foot before…

In the meantime, he has some fantastic stories
to tell his friends back in the city!

General Director: Gauthier Auzou
Senior Editor: Laura Levy
Layout: Eloïse Jensen
Production Manager: Jean-Christophe Collett
Production: Virginie Champeaud
Project Management for the present edition: Ariane Laine-Forrest
Proofreading: Rebecca Frazer
Translation from French: Susan Allen Maurin
Original title: Léon le raton part découvrir le monde

Printed and made in China, February 2016
ISBN : 978-2-7338-4182-2